Doctor Foster went to Gloucester

Retold by Russell Punter

Illustrated by David Semple

Doctor Foster
went to Gloucester,

in a shower of rain.

He stepped in a puddle,

right up to his middle,

and never went there again.

Doctor Foster went to Oxford,

in a cloud of fog.

He just couldn't see,

bumped into a tree

and **splat!** He fell into a bog.

Doctor Foster went to Gosport,

in a howling gale.

The wind was so strong,

it blew him along,

and he flew down the street with a wail.

Doctor Foster went to Stockton,

in the swirling snow.

The frost bit his nose,

his spectacles froze,

and he couldn't see which way to go.

Doctor Foster went to Bognor,

in the sizzling heat.

He took off his socks,

fell asleep on some rocks,

and got sunburned all over his feet.

Doctor Foster's rounds are over,
and he's home once more.

Now his work is complete,
he can put up his feet.

"It's much safer here, that's for sure."

Edited by Lesley Sims

First published in 2015 by Usborne Publishing Ltd., Usborne House, 83-85 Saffron Hill,
London EC1N 8RT, England. www.usborne.com Copyright © 2015 Usborne Publishing Ltd.